This book belongs to:

Disney's 5-minute ADVENTURE Stories

Written by Sarah Heller
Illustrated by the Disney Storybook Artists
Designed by the Disney Global Design Group

Disney PRESS

New York

ISBN: 0-7868-3361-0

Library of Congress Catalog Card Number: 2001095760

Visit www.disneybooks.com

CONTENTS

Buzz to the Rescue!

"There you go, pardners," Andy said as he packed Sheriff Woody, Jessie the cowgirl, and Bullseye the horse into his backpack. Jessie couldn't wait to go to cowboy camp—Woody said there were *real* horses there.

"Almost ready?" Andy's mom asked as she poked her head into his room. Glancing at Andy's half-open backpack, she shook her head. "Andy, you know the rules. Just one toy."

"Oh, all right," Andy said with a sigh. "Sorry, guys." He lifted Jessie and Bullseye out of the bag and placed them on the windowsill.

Jessie and Bullseye watched out the window as Andy walked to the car. Jessie swallowed hard to keep from crying as the car drove away.

Bullseye nuzzled her shoulder, and Jessie patted him on the head.

"I know you're disappointed, too," she said sadly.

Bullseye whinnied as Jessie climbed down from the window and flopped into a box full of books. Andy's mom had just put the box in his room that morning, and Jessie thought its high sides would make a nice, private place. No such luck.

She had only been there a moment when Buzz Lightyear, a Space Ranger toy, poked his head over the side of the box.

"Don't be sad, Jessie," Buzz said, climbing into the box. "You don't need to go to camp to have an adventure. We can have a great time here. Right, guys?"

All of Andy's toys agreed. Rex the dinosaur, Hamm the piggy bank, and Slinky Dog gathered around the box to cheer Jessie up.

"Thank you all," Jessie told her friends, "but I think I'd just like to be alone for a little while."

The toys nodded sadly and left.

Suddenly, a Green Army Man yelled, "Red alert!"

Someone was coming. All of the toys fell lifeless to the floor as Andy's doorknob turned and the baby-sitter walked in.

"I'll be down in a minute, Molly!" the baby-sitter yelled to Andy's little sister.

She looked down at a list in her hand. "Let's see…. 'Put box of old books in attic,'" she read.

Old books, Jessie thought. Oh, no! While the baby-sitter peered at her list, Jesse glanced down at the side of the box. It read: OLD BOOKS.

Jessie was about to be put into storage in the attic!

Jessie lay perfectly still as the baby-sitter turned out the light and closed the attic door. Then she climbed out of the box. "Let me out of here!" she cried.

Jessie pushed and banged on the attic door. It would not budge. Looking around the attic, Jessie spotted a small window. She climbed up on a few boxes so she could look out.

The view was the same as the one from Andy's window—only higher. Jessie realized that Andy's room must be directly below. Suddenly, Jessie had an idea.

Meanwhile, the toys in Andy's room were planning a rescue.

"Okay, recruits, here's the plan," Buzz said as he pointed to Etch A Sketch, who quickly drew a picture of the stairs to the attic.

"The Green Army Men will lead the attack, and radio back if they run into danger. At the top of the stairs, the men will form a pyramid and grab

on to the doorknob,
opening the door," Buzz said.
Etch A Sketch drew quickly to keep up
with his words. "Once the door is open,
I'll go in and get Jessie," Buzz added.

The toys nodded. They all knew
what to do.

"Let's go, everyone!" Buzz cried.
"We've got a toy to save!"

Jessie managed to open an old trunk in
the attic, and began digging around inside.
There were some old newspapers, three
books, a baby blanket, and a jump rope.

A jump rope! Jessie pulled the jump
rope out of the trunk and tied it into a quick
slipknot.

"It's not the best lasso I've ever seen," she said to herself, "but it'll have
to do."

Jessie twirled the makeshift lasso a few times and threw the loop over
the window lock. Then she hauled herself up onto the ledge. She opened the
window a few inches and crawled outside.

"Don't look down," she told herself as she stepped onto the ledge.

Just then, Jessie heard someone fiddling with the attic doorknob. Oh,
no, Jessie thought. The baby-sitter is back! Jessie closed her eyes, grabbed the
rope, and jumped.

"Green Army Men, fall in!" Sarge commanded.

The sergeant gave Buzz a snappy salute, then turned to his men and barked a few commands. Within moments, they had formed a pyramid.

Buzz held his breath as the Green Army Man at the top grabbed the knob. He fumbled with it, but after a moment it turned! The door was open.

"Hang on, Jessie!" Buzz cried as he ran into the attic. "We'll rescue you!"

But Jessie was nowhere to be seen!

Buzz gasped as he looked around and spotted the open window. Scrambling up some old cardboard boxes, Buzz hauled himself out onto the ledge. Looking down, he saw Jessie. She was dangling at the end of a jump rope—it looked as if she were about to fall!

"Don't let go, Jessie!" Buzz shouted. "I'm coming for you!"

Buzz deployed his wings. Then, taking a deep breath, he dove out the window.

Jessie looked up and saw Buzz falling out the attic window—right toward her.

"Look out!" Buzz cried.

Thinking fast, Jessie swung her legs out and caught Buzz just as he was about to fall past her. He was heavy, and the rope jerked under his weight.

"Whoa!" Jessie shouted as she and Buzz swung forward—right through Andy's open window. Hearing the noise, all of Andy's toys ran into the room, to find Buzz and Jessie lying on the floor.

"Are you okay?" Rex asked.

Buzz was the first to sit up. "I'm more than okay!" he crowed. "Our rescue effort was successful, everyone! We saved Jessie!"

Jessie laughed and stood up. "Is that where you

all were—rescuing me? Well, thanks, everybody!" Jessie grinned as she looked around at her good friends. "Even though I didn't get to go to cowboy camp, this has been the best adventure ever! Yee-hah!"

"Yee-hah!" all the toys cheered, welcoming Jessie back to where she belonged.

Puppy Trouble

"**W**e won't be gone long," Pongo promised Perdita. The Dalmatians were joining their human pets, Roger and Anita, for a picnic with old friends. It was a beautiful summer day, and Pongo was excited to get to the park.

"I'm just not sure we should leave the puppies," Perdita said. "Will Nanny be able to handle all fifteen of them by herself?"

Pongo smiled at his little Dalmatians. They were curled up snugly together in their sleeping basket.

"What could possibly go wrong?" he asked Perdita. "The puppies are napping. Besides, Nanny can handle anything."

Perdita
nodded, trying to
forget her worries as
she followed Pongo into
the sunshine. Pongo is right, she
told herself firmly—the puppies will be
absolutely fine.

It was not long before the puppies started
to yawn and stretch. Rolly's paw hit Lucky in the
ear, waking him.

The smell of fresh summer air made Lucky
want to go outside. "Let's get Nanny to take us for a
walk!" Lucky urged the other puppies.

When Nanny finished watering the plants, she
turned and saw fifteen puppies eagerly holding their leashes
in their mouths. "Oh, dear," she said, looking into their big,
hopeful eyes. "Well, I suppose puppies do need to go for a
walk now and then."

With seven leashes in her right hand and eight in her left,
Nanny followed the puppies onto the sidewalks of London. Lucky
strained against his leash as they neared the playground. He couldn't
wait to play on the slide!

When they reached the playground, Nanny unhooked their leashes and
breathed a sigh of relief as the puppies scampered off to play. The puppies
had a wonderful time at the playground. Patch and Pepper loved digging in
the sandbox. Rolly found a rope to chew.

Lucky spotted a pretty butterfly. He got ready to pounce, but the butterfly flew up high and landed on the steps to a slide. Lucky chased the butterfly up the steps, all the way to the top.

The butterfly landed on a nearby wall. Lucky jumped from the top of the slide and landed next to the butterfly, but it flew away again. "Look at me!" Lucky barked happily. "I'm taller than everyone else!"

But his brothers and sisters didn't hear him. They were busy playing. They were so busy, in fact, that they didn't see Lucky jump from the top of the wall to chase the butterfly and disappear on the other side.

When Lucky jumped off the wall, he didn't land on the ground. Instead, he landed in the back of a fire truck. It started speeding down the road.

Whee-oo! Whee-oo! The sirens blared.

"Woof! Woof!" Lucky barked. "I'm a fire dog!"

Lucky enjoyed his ride, but he was glad when the truck pulled to a stop. He knew he had to get back to the playground.

The firemen were busy getting the ladder from the back of the truck. They ran to a big tree.

"Meow!" Lucky saw that there was a kitten stuck in the tree. He watched one of the firemen climb up the tall ladder, then he jumped off the truck.

"A puppy!" someone said with a squeal. Lucky looked up and saw a little girl with curly red hair, pushing a doll carriage. She reached down and picked him up.

"You can be my new dolly," the little girl said as she tied a bonnet onto Lucky's head and dropped him into the carriage. "I'm going to keep you forever."

Lucky shook his head as hard as he could, but the bonnet would not come off. "Grrr," Lucky growled. He did not like being a doll. Besides, he had to get back to his family!

Suddenly, the little girl spotted something on the ground. "A button!" she cried. She bent down to pick it up. Lucky knew there was no time to lose. He jumped out of the carriage and pawed off the bonnet. Then he ran down the street as fast as he could.

At the end of the block, Lucky cocked his ears and listened. He could hear barking! His brothers and sisters were only a couple of blocks away.

Lucky raced across the street. He heard a horn honk as a car swerved to avoid him, driving into a mud puddle. Dirty water splashed all over Lucky,

but he ran on and on. When he finally made it to the playground, he was out of breath.

Inside the playground, Nanny was trying to count the puppies, but they kept running around.

"Oh, I give up!" she said finally.

"Woof! Woof!" Lucky barked as he scratched eagerly at the gate.

Nanny looked up. "Why, hello, little pup," she said as Lucky wagged his tail. "Too bad you can't come with us. But you're not a Dalmatian. You should go find your own family—I'm sure they're worried about you."

Lucky was confused, but then he caught sight of his reflection in a nearby puddle. He was covered with dirt. He looked like a Labrador puppy— Nanny didn't recognize him!

Lucky realized that he had to wash the mud off his fur right away. He ran to join some children who were playing in a fountain.

The children giggled as the little Dalmatian jumped

about in the fountain, then shook his wet fur. A man sitting on a nearby bench looked over and frowned. He was not happy. His newspaper was covered with water and mud.

Lucky ran toward home. He grinned as he spotted Nanny crouching in front of the house, unhooking his brothers' and sisters' leashes.

"My goodness," she said as Lucky ran past her and into the house. "Where did you come from?"

Later, when Pongo and Perdita came home, they found Lucky curled up in the sleeping basket.

"You see?" Pongo whispered to Perdita. "I told you nothing would go wrong."

Surfing the Jungle

"These bananas are great!" Terk said to Tarzan as they sat munching fruit on the branch of a tall banana tree. "Remember the first time you tried to get your own bananas?"

Tarzan laughed. "How could I forget?" he asked.

Tarzan and Terk smiled as they remembered one day, years before, when they were running through the forest.

"You'll never catch me!" Terk cried as she raced ahead.

Tarzan did his best to keep up, but he had a strange shape for a gorilla, and sometimes it made him slow.

"Don't go so fast," he complained. "Wait for me!"

Suddenly, Terk stopped in her tracks.

Tarzan caught up to her and whispered, "Why did you stop?"

Terk took a deep sniff and grinned. "Can't you smell the bananas?"
she asked.

Tarzan inhaled. He couldn't smell anything, so he shook his head.

Terk sighed, then pointed to the leafy tree that stretched out above them.
Tarzan looked up. He couldn't see anything.

"There aren't any bananas up there," he said, folding his arms across his
chest.

Terk planted her hands on her hips. "Wanna bet?" she asked. Then,
turning to the tree, she scrambled up its thick trunk.

Looking around, Tarzan bit his lip. Terk made it seem as if climbing trees
was easy. But it wasn't, at least not for Tarzan. He ran toward the tree and
jumped, reaching as far as he could in order to catch the lowest branch.

He missed, and fell face first onto the soft ground.

"Tarzan, you are one strange gorilla!" Terk laughed and dropped a banana peel on Tarzan's head. She had reached the top already. There *were* bananas up there!

Tarzan was more eager than ever to follow her—he wanted a banana, not just a peel. But he did not have long arms and strong muscles like Terk.

Tarzan decided to try a different approach. He hugged the tree and tried to inch himself up the trunk. But he didn't really get anywhere. After a few moments he couldn't hold on anymore.

Within seconds, Tarzan fell to the ground. His gorilla mother, Kala, saw him and hurried over. "Why don't you stay with me this afternoon," she suggested, picking up Tarzan and giving him a hug.

Tarzan reached over Kala's shoulder, and grabbed a nearby vine. He used the vine to swing himself onto a low tree branch.

"Terk always says I'm a strange gorilla," Tarzan told his mother, "but I just want to be like everybody else." Balancing carefully, Tarzan stood on the branch and reached for the one just above his head. "That's why

I'm going to climb this tree and get a bunch of bananas—I'll show Terk!"

"Tarzan," Kala said, "you're not strange. You're special."

But Tarzan was barely listening. He was busy pulling himself up onto the next branch.

Tarzan grabbed a higher branch with his fingertips and swung his leg clumsily up and over. All the way up the tree he stretched, swinging and wiggling as he went.

Near the top he inched his way out on a limb toward Terk's tree.

"Ho-hum!" Terk yawned, and threw another banana peel at Tarzan. It missed him and fell to the ground.

Tarzan strained to reach the next branch.

"Chirp, chirp!" Tiny baby birds stretched their necks nervously to peek out of their nest. Tarzan smiled at them.

"Aaah!" Tarzan cried suddenly. A mother bird had just swooped down at him. He stood up, and the thin branch below him swayed.

Remembering the vine he had used to pull himself up to the banana tree, Tarzan reached out and grabbed another vine. He used it to swing to a stronger branch below.

"Oof!" Tarzan grunted as he landed, shaking the whole tree. Just then, he heard a strange buzzing noise coming from a large hole in the tree right in front of him.

Tarzan peeked into the hole, and his jaw dropped at what he saw there. Bees!

Buzz! Buzz! Buzz!

"Aaarrggh!" Tarzan turned and ran along the branch as the angry bees flew out of the hole.

Tarzan's feet slipped and slid. The branch had moss all over it. Tarzan had never noticed it before, but now he realized that many of the trees in

the forest were covered with slippery moss.

He put out his arms to help him keep his balance, but he was still a bit wobbly. He bent his knees, and found that made him steadier.

Whoosh! Tarzan was soon sliding down the tree limb so fast that he left the bees far behind. He felt as if he were flying.

Soon the branch thinned out. Tarzan tried to slow down before he reached the end but he was going too fast. He did not know how to stop himself.

"Help me!" Tarzan cried as he flew right into Terk's tree—but Terk wasn't there anymore. Tarzan landed on another mossy branch and slid past a family of surprised baboons. Then, he hit a bunch of bananas and crashed through the leaves out into the air again. Clutching the bananas to his chest, Tarzan fell to the ground.

He landed right in the middle of his gorilla family, facedown on the bunch of bananas.

"Tarzan, you are one strange gorilla," Terk said.

"Tarzan! Are you okay?" Kala cried. She hurried over and pulled Tarzan to his feet.

"I'm fine," he answered, sheepishly.

Kala smiled. "I see you got those bananas you were looking for," she said, picking a banana out of the bunch. She peeled it and took a big bite. "Delicious!" she exclaimed. "Why, I do believe this is the best banana I have ever tasted! And you've brought back enough for everyone—how thoughtful."

Everyone in Tarzan's family wanted a banana. Kala was right. There was more than enough for everybody!

"Terk never brings us bananas," one of the younger gorillas pointed out.

Terk looked embarrassed. Tarzan laughed.

"Have a banana," he said to her.

Tarzan never forgot what he learned that day. He learned to share with his family. He learned to see himself as special. And he learned how to surf the jungle and travel as quickly as a gorilla.

"Have a banana," the grown-up Tarzan said to Terk, who laughed.

"Tarzan," she said, "you are one special gorilla."

Abu's Adventure

The Magic Carpet swooped through the Agrabah marketplace.

"Abu! Stop covering my eyes!" Aladdin cried as he tried to pry the monkey's arms from around his head. "How can I find a gift for the Genie when I can't see?"

Abu didn't let go. The Magic Carpet was speeding between the stalls. Suddenly, the Carpet stopped short. Aladdin disentangled himself from Abu's grip as he hopped off the Carpet.

"Thanks, Carpet." Aladdin gave the rug a high five on one of its tassels.

Abu followed Aladdin and the Carpet to a stall that was packed with interesting things. Although they had been to the marketplace a hundred times, none of them had ever seen this stall before.

"May I help you?" asked the merchant in the stall. He was tall and very thin, and his eyes were a strange yellow color.

"What's this?" Aladdin asked as he picked up an unusual blue tube.

"Hold it to the light, and you will see the changing colors of the rainbow," the merchant replied.

As the merchant talked to Aladdin, Abu climbed up the side of the stall. Wrapping his tail around a pole, Abu lowered himself so that he was directly above Aladdin's head. Then he plucked off Aladdin's hat and put it on his own head.

Some people nearby laughed and threw fruit to Abu. Still suspended from the bar, Abu juggled three apples.

"What a clever little monkey you have," the merchant said to Aladdin.

Aladdin turned to look at Abu.

"Give that back!" he cried, snatching his hat from Abu. "Sometimes he's a little *too* clever," he said to the merchant.

"Perhaps I could buy him from you?" the merchant said. "I also run a troupe of traveling acrobats."

"Sorry," Aladdin replied. "This monkey may be trouble, but he's not for sale."

"I understand," the merchant said.

Although the merchant had many wonderful things on display, none of his wares seemed quite right for the Genie, so Aladdin turned to look at another stall.

The Carpet followed him.

Aladdin searched stand after stand, with no luck.

Finally, Aladdin held up an oversized yellow robe. "What do you think of this?" he asked, turning to show it to Abu. "I think the yellow—" Aladdin stopped in midsentence.

"Abu?" Aladdin called. He looked around, but there was no sign of Abu. "Oh, no," Aladdin said to himself. "Abu is angry because I yelled at him. Now he's run away. Come on, Carpet!"

Aladdin and the Carpet flew through the marketplace in search of their friend.

"Abu, where are you?" Aladdin cried. But there was no response.

Abu had disappeared!

A few days later, the Genie

appeared
in the Sultan's
palace.

"Al! Hey, Al!" the
Genie shouted. "You'll
never believe what I saw!" Suddenly,
he noticed Aladdin's expression. "Hey, why
the long face?" he asked.

Aladdin sighed. "I yelled at Abu, and he ran away."

"Ran away?" The Genie scratched his head.
"That's funny, because I went to see this troupe
of acrobats," he said. "They had a monkey that
looked just like Abu! The monkey flipped through
the air, then hung by his tail from a high wire and juggled
four apples."

Aladdin frowned. He was
becoming very uneasy. "You said he
looked just like Abu?" he asked.

The Genie nodded. "He
could have been Abu's twin!"

Suddenly, Aladdin
remembered something that
the man in the marketplace
had said to him just before Abu
disappeared—"I also run a troupe
of traveling acrobats."

"That was no twin!" Aladdin cried, grabbing the Genie by the shoulders. "Genie, Abu didn't run away—he's been monkey-napped! And we've got to save him!"

Meanwhile, Abu sat huddled in a cage. "It's show time!" Abu heard a low voice say. He turned around and saw two yellow eyes looking in at him. It was the merchant.

Abu tried to crawl into a corner, remembering how the merchant had shoved him into a sack when Aladdin turned his back in the marketplace. But the merchant was too quick. He grabbed Abu and perched him on his shoulder.

"Now, you'll perform like the clever little monkey you are, won't you?" the merchant asked.

Abu stuck out his tongue at the evil merchant.

The merchant frowned. "You'll do it, or there will be no dinner for you tonight!"

Abu sighed. He just *had* to find a way to escape!

The Genie and Aladdin flew high over the desert on the Magic Carpet. They had already been to the town where the Genie had seen Abu, but the acrobats had moved on. Nobody knew where they had gone.

"There!" the Genie cried at last.

Aladdin looked down and saw a bright red tent set up in the middle of an oasis. The acrobats were performing in there!

"To the red tent, Carpet," Aladdin said.

The Magic Carpet swooped down toward the oasis.

Aladdin, the Genie, and the Carpet took their seats inside the tent.

After a moment, the lights went down. Then Abu appeared—perched on the high wire!

Aladdin gasped. "Abu!" he shouted. "Be careful!"

The crowd turned to look at Aladdin. "Seize him!" cried the merchant.

As two guards ran toward Aladdin, he and the Genie hopped onto the

Magic Carpet and zoomed toward Abu.

"Grab the monkey!" the merchant shouted, and two of the acrobats began inching out onto the high wire toward Abu.

For a moment, Abu stood in the middle of the high wire, not moving. He knew that if the acrobats caught him, he'd have to go back to his cage. Finally, Abu made a decision. He closed his eyes and jumped.

"Gotcha!" Aladdin cried as Abu landed safely in his arms. The audience cheered.

Aladdin had forgotten that he was in the middle of a crowd, but Abu knew just what to do. He waved, then stuck out his tongue at the angry merchant as he flew away with his friends, free at last.

Ariel and the Sea-Horse Race

King Triton, ruler of all the oceans, stormed through the palace courtyard.

"*Ariel!*" His voice thundered.

The young mermaid appeared, riding her sea horse, Stormy.

"Daddy, I know what you are going to say—" Ariel began, but King Triton interrupted his daughter, waving a scroll angrily.

"Ariel, how could you sign up for the Annual Sea-Horse Race?" he asked. "It's a dangerous competition! No mermaid has ever competed in this race."

Ariel raised her chin defiantly. "Mermaids ride sea horses, too, Daddy," she said. "And Stormy may be small, but he's fast. I know we can win that race if you'll only give us a chance."

"You take too many chances!" King Triton shouted.

"But, Daddy . . ." Ariel pleaded.

"No, Ariel. I forbid you to enter the race!" he said.

Ariel knew there was no point in arguing with her

father anymore. With tears in her eyes, she and Stormy slowly made their
way out of the palace courtyard.

Ariel moped around the racecourse all week long. Her best friend,
Flounder, tried to cheer her up.

"That old sea-horse trophy isn't so great, anyway," said Flounder. "Why
don't we go exploring for human stuff?"

But for once, Ariel didn't want to look for human treasures. She only
had one thing on her mind.

"It just isn't fair!" she exclaimed. "I know I could win!"

"Yes," agreed Flounder. "If you were a merman, your father would let
you sign up."

"That's it!" cried Ariel. "I'll be a merman—Arrol, the merman! Flounder,
you're a genius!"

Ariel swam around the palace, looking for a racing uniform and helmet. As she turned a corner, she swam smack into her father's adviser, Sebastian the crab.

"Teenagers," muttered Sebastian. "Always in a hurry."

"Sorry, Sebastian," said Ariel. "I guess I just had racing on my mind."

"You and your father both," Sebastian said as he adjusted his shell. "He keeps going to the closet to look at his old racing uniform. You know, he was just your age when he entered his first competition."

Ariel was surprised. King Triton had never told her that he used to race.

"Thanks, Sebastian!" said Ariel. Now she knew just where to find a racing uniform!

On the morning of the competition, Ariel hid with Stormy near the starting line, her tail swishing back and forth nervously.

Just then, the trumpets sounded. King Triton raised his trident. Quickly, Ariel swung herself onto Stormy's back and urged the

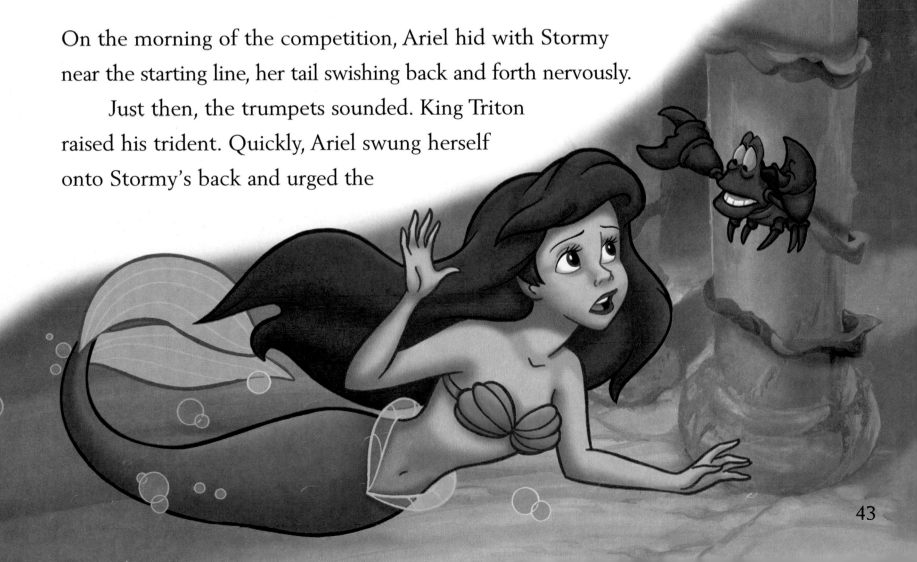

sea horse to the starting line, where they joined the other contestants.

A spark shot out of the tip of Triton's trident. The racers steered their sea horses through the water at breakneck speed. When they reached the coral reef, many of the fastest and more powerful sea horses could not fit through the small openings and had to swim around the coral reef.

But Stormy was small and Ariel was brave. They zipped in and out of the spiky coral. It was not long before they had taken the lead.

"YAHOO!" Ariel shouted with joy. Her cry gave Stormy a burst of energy. The sea horse whipped around the next turn. But this time he was too fast! Ariel's helmet hit the coral and popped off. Her long red hair streamed out behind her.

Ariel's heart was pounding with excitement and fear. Behind her, the mermen were gaining speed.

One racer, Carpa, saw Ariel before she dove into the dark cavern. "A mermaid!" he roared, and urged his powerful sea horse to top speed.

It was pitch-black in the cavern, but Ariel and Stormy knew the way. They had been there before, searching for treasures.

Suddenly, Ariel and Stormy were pushed roughly from behind. Ariel clung tightly to Stormy, but they were pushed again.

"What was that?" Ariel cried, as she pulled Stormy back on course. She turned around. It was Carpa!

Stormy was frightened. He raced ahead and swam out of the cavern at

record speed. He headed for the last part of the racecourse: the seaweed hurdles.

Ariel and Stormy swam over and under the seaweed hurdles. All of Atlantica could see them now. The crowd gasped as everyone recognized King Triton's youngest daughter. The Sea King rose from the royal box, a look of utter surprise on his regal face.

"You haven't won yet, mermaid!" came a rough voice behind Ariel, as Carpa pulled up beside her.

"Neither have you!" Ariel cried, urging Stormy on.

With one last burst of speed, Stormy raced across the finish line.

"Hooray!" cried Ariel's sisters. Flounder did flips as the spectators roared their approval.

Ariel smiled broadly and waved. Then she caught sight of her father. He was looking at her sternly.

Nervously, Ariel steered Stormy toward the royal box. There stood King Triton, holding the gleaming trophy.

"Daddy, I . . ." Ariel began, but she never finished her sentence because King Triton had enveloped her in a giant hug.

"Oh, Ariel, I'm sorry I was so unreasonable," he said. "I had forgotten

how much fun racing could be. All I thought about was how dangerous it was for you to be in a competition like this one. Will you ever forgive your stubborn father?"

Ariel nodded and kissed his rough cheek. Then, proudly, King Triton handed his daughter—the first mermaid ever to win the Annual Sea-Horse Race—her trophy.